owl

bat

pig

fox

porcupine

pangolin

bush baby

woodpecker

For John (my hero), Milo, and Linda
Plus Caz, Caroline & Tanya

The author would like to thank Nyaboke Nyakoe from the Kenya High Commission
for her help in doing research for this book. Also, the keepers of Exmoor Zoo
who enticed their sleepy bat-eared foxes out with mealworms and
enabled her to hear squabbling porcupines rattling their quills.

The wild creatures depicted in this book are the bushpig, bat-eared fox, African porcupine,
yellow-winged bat, tree pangolin, lesser bush baby, spotted eagle-owl, and Nubian woodpecker.

The children in this book are from the Luo people of southwest Kenya.

First U.S. edition 2020

Library of Congress Catalog Card Number pending
ISBN 978-1-5362-1489-5 (hardcover)
ISBN 978-1-5362-1109-2 (paperback)

20 21 22 23 24 25 CCP 10 9 8 7 6 5 4 3 2 1

Printed in Shenzhen, Guangdong, China

This book was typeset in ITC Garamond Book.
The illustrations were done in watercolor.

Candlewick Press
99 Dover Street
Somerville, Massachusetts 02144

visit us at www.candlewick.com

Handa's Noisy Night

Eileen Browne

CANDLEWICK PRESS

Handa arrived to spend the night
with her friend Akeyo.

"Mom says we can sleep in the hut," said Akeyo.

"That will be fun!" said Handa.

"Good night," said Akeyo's mom and dad.

"Sleep tight," said her grandma and granddad.

The girls took sweet corn and toys to the hut.

Handa was really excited.

"I can hear snorting!" said Handa.

"It's Dad," said Akeyo.

"He snorts when he laughs."

snort
snort

"What's that chattering?" said Handa.

"Just the grown-ups," said Akeyo.

"Talking and talking."

chatter
chatter

"Now there's rattling!" said Handa.

"Don't worry," said Akeyo.

"It's Mom, playing the shaker."

rattle

rattle

"Something's squeaking!" said Handa.

"That's Granddad," said Akeyo.

"Riding his rusty old bike."

"Can you hear slurping?" said Handa.

"Yes." Akeyo yawned.

"Grandma's drinking her bedtime milk."

"Oh, no — someone's crying!" said Handa.

"Only my . . . baby sister,"

said Akeyo, falling asleep.

waa!
waa!

Thud!

"What's that?" Handa held her breath.

"Maybe it's . . . a door slamming."

Handa closed her eyes. "Night night, Akeyo."

Next morning, Handa woke to a *tap-tap-tapping*.
"Someone's at the door," said Akeyo. "Come in!"

"That's funny," said Handa. "There's no one here."

"Hello!" said Akeyo's mom. "Did you sleep well?"

"Not really," said Akeyo.

"You were all too noisy!"

"We were quiet as mice," said the grown-ups.

"Oh!" said Handa.

"So *who* was making the noise?"

woodpeck

owl

pig

porcupine

pangolin

fox

bat

bush baby